The Fairfield Triangle

Johnny Ray Barnes, Jr.

A
MONTAGE
PUBLICATION

Montage Publications, a Front Line Company,
San Diego, California

ISBN 1-56714-058-0

Printed in the U.S.A.

TO WILLIAM B.

1

The Fairfield Triangle had claimed no victims in over three years. That is, until Dwayne Barker's unfortunate experience.

Standing in the middle of the open field believed to be the center of the Triangle, Dwayne framed the perfect shot. He took his time setting up a picture he felt would best depict the area's eeriness to his readers.

"It happened right here, thirty-eight months ago," Dwayne muttered to himself. He looked through his camera lens, focused on the spot from which the campsite had mysteriously vanished, and snapped the photo.

Grabbing a small notepad from his back pocket, Dwayne quickly scrawled an entry.

"Shot 24—reported area of the campsite

disappearance by Scout Troop 393," he read aloud as he wrote. "Note to add in quotation marks *'even the ashes from the campfire were missing.'* "

He grinned slightly as he wrote the last words, remembering Scout Ben Huggins' eyewitness account of the vanishing.

I wouldn't lie to you, Mr. Barker. We came out of the woods and it was gone! All gone! Even the ashes from the campfire were missing! And we had only been gone thirty minutes!

In his thirty-nine years, Dwayne had collected many stories like young Ben's. Some of them proved unexplainable. This one, however, seemed to be no big mystery. Dwayne believed the naïve scouts were not the victims of a strange other-worldly disappearance—but a prank.

Just a prank, Dwayne thought, considering whether or not to state that opinion in his book.

He shoved the notepad back into his pocket, set his camera to rewind, and began collecting his things.

Then he noticed something odd occurring across the field where he had parked.

The headlights on his truck . . . *the headlights were flashing*.

Rapidly at first, but then they slowed to a steady pulse, almost like a heartbeat.

"What in the world?" Dwayne mumbled. He tried to look through the windshield, but couldn't see anyone inside.

The flashes continued.

Dwayne headed for the vehicle. The light bursts matched him step for step. As he walked faster, the blinks increased. When he started to run, they practically strobed.

A sudden chill ran up his spine, causing him to stop just before he reached the truck.

"WHO'S IN THERE?" Dwayne yelled.

No one answered.

He stepped closer, straining his neck to look inside. The cab *appeared* empty, but he needed to be certain.

He grabbed the door handle, his sweaty palm struggling for a firm grip. Every muscle tensed. *Then he jerked the door open and . . .*

"Nothing," Dwayne breathed with relief, his blood pressure lowering. "I must have a short in the wiring or something."

Reaching in, he popped the hood for a quick look. As he walked around to check the battery, his eyes caught something moving in the sideview mirror.

Something bright.

It blinded him temporarily. Rubbing his eyes, he leaned against the truck.

In that moment of darkness, he felt a change in the air.

An odd sensation washed over him.

A tingly feeling, like a rippling electric blanket thrown over his back. Every hair on his body stood up. His heart fluttered.

He couldn't be sure, but he thought he felt . . . *a presence.*

Something seething. Curling. Spreading itself over the field in front of him. He couldn't see it, *but he felt it.*

Then his vision returned . . . *and Dwayne Barker screamed.*

2

"The scene of the crime is just ahead of us," said the Sheriff. "I know you want to examine every inch of it, but bear in mind, that is *my* job and anything you touch could contaminate valuable evidence."

"No problem, Dad," Russell Drake answered. The sandy-blonde haired boy sat beside his father in the car, wearing his signature black T-shirt and tightly clutching a leather bag in his arms.

The scene of the crime.

The words rolled through Russell's head like a New Year's Day parade. A crime—reported directly to his father, Sheriff Drake, by its frazzled victim. This time, unlike the hundred or so *other* crimes Russell had begged to help solve, his father agreed to let him have a crack at it.

And it seemed like a brain-buster . . .

The patrol car pulled off the road just beyond Potter's Field, making its way over the scattered gravel that served as crude pavement. Sheriff Drake steered through the narrow winding path, coming ever-so-close to the deep muddied ditches lining the crooked trail. After a few turns, the gravel ended, and the mud took over.

"We'll have to make this quick," said the Sheriff, decreasing his speed to roll over the mud. "If it rains while we're out here, we'll have big trouble making it over this road again."

"If we get stuck, Mr. Barker can help pull us out. He drives that huge Explorer," Russell said, noticing his father's head shaking.

"Mr. Barker's not meeting us here. He's giving a seminar in Mullinfield. I told him I would come up here and give the place a look-over. Of course, I warned him—spontaneous, purposeless crimes like these are the hardest to solve."

Mr. Barker was better known as Dwayne Barker, renowned photographer and author, whose books dealt strictly with subjects of the unknown. His books about the mysteries of the world had made him one of Fairfield's most notable natives. Late yesterday afternoon, Mr. Barker had experienced what he called an "unexplained encounter."

After investigating some faulty wiring under the hood of his truck, the author claimed to have been approached by a bright light. For the next few seconds, everything went black. Then, Mr. Barker reported, he felt waves of electricity humming through him, but in a very soothing way. They practically entranced him. When he finally snapped out of it, he discovered all of his photography equipment was missing: a brand new camera, expensive high-speed lenses, and antique equipment bags—everything—*gone*.

Mr. Barker wanted to cry as he drove home in the rain. He rang the Sheriff's house from his cellular phone.

Across town, Russell was sitting on the couch trying to read *The Hound of the Baskervilles* (his latest Sherlock Holmes tale) when a frantic Dwayne Barker's call came through. He listened as his father urged Mr. Barker to calm down. With keen interest, Russell pieced the problem together as the Sheriff continually repeated Mr. Barker's story in order to understand the situation. When his father hung up the phone, Russell wasted no time in offering to help.

His father accepted, and Russell ran to his room to get his *investigation kit*.

At first glance, the kit looked like a catch-all drawer. The materials in it were everyday items found in any home. But in Russell's kit, each tool had its own special story and purpose.

A magnifying glass for examining the smallest of clues. He had received it as a gift at Christmas from his father, who had purchased it from a collector. It was the actual magnifying glass used in the movie, *Young Sherlock Holmes*.

A refillable notebook for recording clues. Its cover had been signed by Peter Falk—*Columbo* himself!

A flashlight and pocketknife. Given to Russell the day he entered Scouts, they were the same flashlight and pocketknife the Sheriff had used when *he* was a scout.

The rest of the kit contained items less nostalgic, but high in importance: fingerprint powder (made from charcoal), small artists' paintbrushes (for applying fingerprint powder), a pair of tweezers (used for lifting small clues like hair or fabric), a roll of transparent tape (for lifting fingerprints—an art Russell had just mastered), a packet of envelopes (for putting clues into), small baggies (also for clues), colored chalk (for marking clue locations), sheets of tracing paper (to trace footprints or tire tracks), and a tape measure because . . . *you just never know.*

The kit was Russell's most treasured possession, for without his tools, Russell couldn't do his job—*solving crimes.*

Though innocently at first, the obsession arose early in his life. He and his father used to watch the detective shows on television, guessing the villain's identity and motive with each clue that was revealed. Russell kept score. After a couple of seasons, he out-solved his father eight times out of ten. Things went on from there. To Russell's delight, mysteries evolved out of everyday situations. What student drew an unflattering picture of the teacher on the blackboard? Which neighborhood dog dug up his mother's new rose bush? Who ate the last piece of blackberry pie? The questions kept presenting themselves, and Russell wanted to answer them all.

Then the weird things started happening. *Strange things* that occurred every month or so.

His father came home describing crazy reports of zombies, man-eating plants, ghosts, and other supernatural things. The evidence to these reports always came up inconclusive, and the web of mysteries drew Russell in like a fly. He made these "supernatural encounters" his top priority, and, with the exception of his father, he believed he was the only one on the case.

Then he read about Mr. Barker's new book. *The Supernatural Secrets of Fairfield.*

Mr. Barker wanted to turn the camera on his own hometown and record all of its whispered legends. That's what had brought him to the Triangle the day his equipment disappeared.

"So, Dad, do you believe in the legend?" Russell asked.

"The legend? Which one's that?" the Sheriff asked back, knowing full-well the answer to his question.

"You know which one. You're driving straight into it. *The Fairfield Triangle.*"

The Sheriff shook his head again.

"Don't buy into that, son. The Fairfield Triangle's nothing but a joke made up by a bunch of teenagers in the '70s."

"But I hear a lot of adults talking about it, too," Russell remarked.

"Who do you think those teenagers grew up to be?" the Sheriff shot back.

"Was Mr. Barker one of them?" Russell asked.

"I don't know. Maybe. He wanted to make the Fairfield Triangle a big chapter in his book, which makes me wonder if this isn't just some kind of publicity stunt," grumbled the Sheriff as he turned the wheel one final time, curving the car over the top of a hill, where they came to a stop.

In front of them lay an open field. Its tall grass swayed, moving like waves in a green ocean. Towering trees surrounded the vast rippling circle, insuring its privacy from the outside world.

"Kind of nice, isn't it?" the Sheriff asked, leaning back and soaking in the view.

Russell watched the grass dance. It almost seemed to motion for them, begging them to visit. For as long as he could remember, Fairfield had brimmed with frightening tales of things disappearing in the terrible Triangle. Now, as he sat staring at its heart, it looked . . . *pleasant*.

"Let's go have a look around," said Russell, feeling uncontrollably drawn to its mystery.

Drawn like a fly once again. Not into a web this time, but into an enormous, ever-waiting black hole.

A geographic Venus Fly Trap.

The Fairfield Triangle.

3

Russell stepped out of the car into an enormous puddle of mud, soaking his shoes. Never one to gripe, moan, or whine, he simply trudged through it, leaving his father behind.

"Son, wait a minute. It's a very delicate area. Let me lead the way in case we come across something."

"Yes, sir," Russell answered, then stopped.

Looking down, he saw Mr. Barker's tire tracks. They ran like a wet noodle across the trail. When the author tore out of the area, he definitely had trouble controlling his vehicle.

"Mr. Barker must've really been mad. Or spooked," the Sheriff said, walking up beside his son.

"Yeah, maybe," Russell answered.

The Sheriff raised a brow.

"Maybe?" he asked. "What do *you* think happened here?"

"Well, Dad, as you know, proof is always our goal. Without proof, we're not even sure a crime has taken place here. But I think I just found evidence proving that someone else besides Mr. Barker showed up here yesterday. Mr. Barker came to take pictures, right?"

"That's what he said," the Sheriff answered.

"It seems unlikely that he took pictures in the rain."

"He didn't. It began to rain *after* his equipment vanished."

"Okay. Hmmm . . . Mr. Barker seemed pretty wound-up when he talked to you on the phone."

"That he was . . . "

"So he must have just fled the scene when he called our house."

"That's correct. Otherwise, he would've had time to calm down a bit."

"Then if it wasn't raining while he took the pictures, it couldn't have been raining when he walked to his truck. And if it was, it must have just started."

"True, true . . . "

14

"He said he turned around and saw his equipment missing once he reached his truck. If that's the exact point in time when he panicked, then that's when he jumped into his truck and left the scene. Seconds later, he called you."

"I see what you're getting at. There was no time for it to rain hard enough to muddy the trail this badly. Therefore, these could not be Mr. Barker's tracks."

"Correct."

"I like your thinking, son. Good deductive reasoning. But think for a second. If you turned around and found all your expensive camera equipment gone, wouldn't you take a few moments to search for it?"

"More than likely . . . "

"And after a few minutes, it starts to rain, but you haven't looked hard enough yet, so you keep searching and searching. Your heart rate jumps, you become more and more excited and confused because you can't find your stuff. Then, when you've exhausted yourself over how something can just vanish off the face of the earth, *that's* when you run to your truck and hightail it for help. See, son, you have to consider the actions of a very curious, very scared individual."

"That's true, Dad. I didn't think about that. But still, I have physical evidence."

"Physical evidence?"

"Oh, yeah. You see, before we left home, I called the Ford dealership. I got one of the salesmen to make an etching of an Explorer's tires and fax it over to me."

"Car salesmen will do that . . . ?"

Russell reached into his kit and pulled out a folded piece of paper. He unfolded it and held it next to the tire track in the mud.

"Sure. Car salesmen are always there to help. These tracks come from a different vehicle, assuming that Mr. Barker still has factory tires. And besides, they lead the other way . . . *into* the Triangle."

The Sheriff shook his head, unable to respond. Russell pulled out a clean piece of paper and some charcoal from his backpack, and carefully made an etching of the tracks. When he finished, he gently folded his evidence and put it in his pocket.

The Sheriff followed the tracks, motioning for Russell to stick with him.

As the tire tracks ran into the open field, they became increasingly wild. The turns curved wider, kicking up more mud. Whoever drove the vehicle wanted one thing: *to tear up mud.*

The two of them followed the crazy tracks until they suddenly stopped near the center of the field.

"This is . . . strange," the Sheriff said, pointing to the trail's end."

"I think I know what you mean," Russell answered. "There's no mud raised in the opposite direction."

"Right. Traveling the speed these tracks imply, the driver would have had to throw his brakes on hard to stop like this. That would've kicked mud up in the opposite direction."

Russell dug into his bag and pulled out his magnifying glass. Bending down, he examined the tracks' stopping point.

He could see nothing unusual at first—mashed blades of grass rolled up in the dirt, tiny worms freeing themselves from the thick, brown muck, and a bottlecap.

"Dad. Bottlecap. Loopy Cola," Russell deadpanned.

"Hmmm . . . Loopy Cola. Now that's a beverage you don't see much. I used to love that stuff. I think Reynold's Pharmacy gets some in every now and then," the Sheriff remarked, glancing down for a second before turning to take a long look around the field.

"Do you think it's important?" Russell asked.

"A bottlecap's not going to solve this case, son."

Russell pulled a handkerchief from his kit, picked up the bottlecap, and dropped it into a little plastic baggie. Then he turned it over and read the underside of it.

"It says 'You're a triple winner. Three times the regular prize,' Dad," Russell said.

"TRIPLE WINNER? Let me see that!" The Sheriff exclaimed. Russell handed it to him. "Well, I'll be . . . you've got yourself thirty bucks there, son. Don't spend it all in one place!"

As he handed the baggie back to Russell, something loud rustled in the woods at the edge of the field.

"What's that?" Russell asked.

"Stay back," the Sheriff warned, pushing Russell behind him with his hand.

Sheriff Drake moved forward cautiously, as the noises in the woods became louder. He walked toward the brush, deftly slipping his billy club from its side snap. As he got closer, he held the club in the air ready to strike.

Russell's heart quickly rose to his throat, pumping frantically, making it difficult for him to breathe. Suddenly, he felt light as a feather. Setting his kit on the ground, he silently walked behind his dad, *determined to help*, he told himself. Deep down, he knew he just didn't want to be left there alone. If anything did spring out of those woods, he wanted to be near his dad and that billy club.

Then Russell saw a light—revealing two very large eyes.

"DAD, LOOK OUT!" Russell screamed.

Too late.

The owl streaked from the trees, passed the spinning Sheriff Drake, and sailed into the air toward the thicket on the other side of the field.

Russell watched it land, then looked to his dad, who had turned very pale.

"Well . . . do you think *that's* the thing behind all this?" the Sheriff asked.

Russell grinned. "I don't think even the wise old owl's smart enough to pull this one off. So, where was Mr. Barker's equipment when it disappeared?"

The Sheriff slid his billy club back into the

holder on his belt.

"A few yards down, where the scouts faked that campsite disappearance. He was taking pictures there."

Russell turned around to grab his kit—

"Whoa," he exclaimed.

"Whoa, what?" the Sheriff asked.

"My kit," said Russell.

"What about your kit?"

"It's . . . *gone!*"

4

"We'll come back later and find your kit, I promise," the Sheriff told Russell as they drove home in the rain.

"WHY COULDN'T WE STAY? WE DIDN'T EVEN CHECK THE WOODS THAT WELL!" Russell agonized, pressing his palm against his forehead to keep from smashing his head into the dashboard out of desperation.

"It started to pour, son! I'm not keeping you out in the rain to catch pneumonia, no matter what you lost! We'll come back tomorrow and search for it. Some animal probably dragged it off into the woods. Raccoons do things like that all the time!"

"Dad! You don't understand!" Russell whined. Russell *never* whined.

His dad turned and looked at him with a

stone face—fair warning to his son.

Russell buried his face in his hands, trying to massage a reason from his brain for his horrible misfortune. That kit—his investigation kit, the tools of his profession, the devices he had become so dependent upon—was irreplaceable. Nothing else he had ever owned had been with him as long, and no possession ever meant more. Now he felt helpless. Powerless . . .

No. What was he thinking? He had rolled the woeful question, *why me?* around in his head over and over again. In his anguish, he forgot to apply one of the detective's basic rules. *Always flip the question.*

Why *not* him?

Suddenly, the answer to his soul-wrenching dilemma became obvious.

I've been challenged, Russell thought.

In the face of his biggest mystery to date, his weapons had been stripped from him. It would be the ultimate test of his skills: to solve the mystery of the Fairfield Triangle *and* recover his investigation kit.

This revelation calmed Russell quickly, and he began to think in a more deductive way.

"Dad, I'm sorry," he said.

"That's quite okay, son. I know how upset you are," the Sheriff answered, turning his windshield wipers to low as the rain died off.

"Dad, I need to go to the library."

"The library's not open, son. It closed at six."

An investigative roadblock. Russell rethought his options.

"Then how about the video store?" Russell asked.

The Sheriff glanced over and saw the hound dog expression on his son's face.

"Okay. We'll stop by there and pick up something. Hey, I hear *Married to the Badge* is in . . ."

The video store looked unusually uncrowded. Once inside, the Sheriff perused the new releases wall while Russell stuck to the documentaries. He had often praised the store for its vast informative library of nonfictional subjects. Every so often, Russell needed an answer for one of his many puzzles after the library had closed its doors. In such cases, he would sometimes refer to this video aisle. This time, he felt certain he would find what he needed.

"X marks the spot," he muttered, finding the title he sought.

Secrets of the Bermuda Triangle.

Russell sighed in relief. Finally, a tool with which to begin his investigation. He faced an area into which many things disappeared, so why not compare it to the most famous case? It might give him some new direction for an examination.

As he reached for the box, another hand shot forward and snatched the video right off the shelf.

"Excuse me . . ." Russell began.

"Yeah?" asked a girl whose jaw smacked on a piece of gum.

"Crystal Barker," Russell muttered. One of Dwayne Barker's triplet daughters. The *mean* one.

"Russell Drake. Well whatdaya know," she answered in a smart-alecky tone.

"I was going to rent that," said Russell, reaching to grab the tape from her hand.

Crystal's hand shot into the air, holding the video behind her back. "No way, greedy, my dad wants this one. Besides, I grabbed it first. Take a hike."

Russell's head began to heat up, and steam practically erupted from his ears. "I . . . need . . .

that . . . tape . . .," he seethed.

"I . . . don't . . . care . . .," she mimicked.

"Hi, Russell," someone else said.

Down the aisle walked Brenna, another Barker sister. The *nice* one. Except for a few differences, she looked exactly like her sister. The Barker sisters always wore red, but Brenna sported long sleeves rather than a T-shirt like Crystal. Each girl also had brunette hair, though Crystal's looked wild and curly while Brenna's hung straight.

"What's going on?" Brenna asked.

"It's your sister," Russell said. "She's being evil."

"I've gotta be me," she said. "Come on, Brenna, let's go."

"Russell-Russell-Bo-Bussell, Banana-Fanna-Fo-Fussell," another voice rang out.

Russell, Crystal, and Brenna suddenly looked confused, until they saw Addy, the third of the Barker triplets (hair in a ponytail, red skirt and sweatshirt), making the rhyme. Everyone knew her as the weird one.

"RUSSELL! Russell . . . *Russell?* Is everything okay? I see you're in the 'Self Help' section," Addy asked with concern.

Russell groaned.

"I wasn't looking on that shelf. I was looking on this one," he said, pointing to the documentaries. "And I found the video I wanted, then Cruella DeVil here snatched it up."

Crystal stuck out her tongue.

"You wanted to see the Bermuda Triangle video, too?" Brenna asked. "That's weird. Our father sent us in to get it for him. He's waiting out in the car."

"I thought your dad was out of town," Russell replied.

"He came back early," Brenna explained. "He's been kind of edgy. Did you know his camera equipment disappeared yesterday, right in the middle of the Fairfield Triangle?"

"Oh, yeah. That's where my dad and I just came from. And your father's not the only one to lose something there. My whole investigation kit just vanished into thin air," Russell told them.

Crystal snorted a chuckle, but Brenna and Addy felt genuinely sorry for him.

"Did you see anything take it? What happened?" Brenna asked.

"My back was turned at the time, but I had hoped to get some clues by watching this video and reading up on the Bermuda Triangle. I figured they might have some common attributes," Russell explained.

"That's what Dad thought, too," Addy said.

"That's what I thought about what?" a deep voice cut in.

Russell looked up to see Dwayne Barker approaching.

Suddenly, Russell felt strangely at ease. Though they differed in many ways, Russell had always felt a certain kinship with Fairfield's most famous writer. He always saw Mr. Barker as an investigator like himself, and although Russell felt he had a higher success rate than Mr. Barker when it came to solving their respective cases, he had always admired the writer's tenacity and desire to keep looking.

"Russell Drake. How are you, son?" Mr. Barker asked, offering his hand to shake. Russell took it and felt its cold clamminess. He noticed that Mr. Barker looked paler than usual, and seemed to be a bit more wound-up.

"Not so good, Mr. Barker," Russell said, explaining his plight in detail. The writer seemed thoroughly interested and hung onto every word. Soon the story became a note-comparing session.

"I think we have similar reasons for wanting to see this video tonight," Mr. Barker said. "I've got an idea. Why don't you come over and watch it with us. Is your dad around? He can come, too."

"Right here, Dwayne," Sheriff Drake answered, patting a copy of *The Patrollers* against his leg. "What's up?"

"We've got a video here everyone wants to see, and I was asking your son if you and he would like to come over and watch it."

"Well, his mother's waiting on us for supper . . ." the Sheriff started. He looked again at Russell's hound dog expression. He'd never seen his son act this way before. "But if Russell's really dying to see it, then I guess I could pick him up at your place later."

"Thanks, Dad," Russell said.

Then Mr. Barker pulled the Sheriff aside to talk about his case. Russell watched them intently, until Crystal broke his concentration.

"So, do you think this tape will tell you where your 'investigation kit' is?" she teased.

Russell grinned in defiance.

"I've found stolen bikes with nothing to go on but a bent blade of grass," Russell remarked.

"And this is a whole video that's full of clues from the first minute to the last. Solving the mystery of the Fairfield Triangle's going to be a piece of cake."

5

Russell felt clueless.

The video had lasted forty-two minutes and went through a lot of information.

The narrator stated that in the last century and a half, over forty ships and at least twenty planes had disappeared inside the Bermuda Triangle. Number of people lost? Almost a thousand.

Then there were the individual cases. With the time allotted, the program only ran through the most famous stories. It began with one of the first: a French ship named the *Rosalie* was found deserted near Nassau in 1840. There were no leaks found in the ship, and its valuable cargo remained undamaged. Someone found a starving canary in a cage, the only living creature on board. Other ships included in the Triangle mystery were the *Belle*, the *Atalanta*, and the *Spray* sailed by Joshua Slocum, the world's best known and most skilled sailor in 1909. He vanished with his boat inside the Triangle.

Then, of course, came Flight 19. On December 5, 1945, five Avenger torpedo bombers disappeared while on a routine patrol over the Bermuda Triangle. This is probably the legend's most famous puzzle, and the documentary examined it in great detail, using close to fifteen of its forty-two minutes.

Then, finally, the narrator got to the theories, Russell's favorite part of any investigation —besides gaining undeniable proof.

The first Bermuda Triangle theory involved *Vile Vortices*. After the large number of disappearances in the Bermuda Triangle and another mysterious zone, The Devil's Sea, some scientists used those areas to map other trouble spots on the globe. To their surprise, each zone proved to be the same distance above the equator, and measured exactly seventy-two degrees apart from each other. Equal distances! Could the Fairfield Triangle be linked to these *Vile Vortices* somehow?

Another theory involved *Magnetic Variation*.

In the Bermuda Triangle, a compass needle points to the true north, unlike most areas where the compass needle will point to the magnetic north. Thus, the hypothesis is that the missing pilots and sailors neglected to adjust their settings, which threw them off course and lost them to the sea. Russell saw no possible connection to this theory and the Fairfield Triangle.

Then came the most sensational theory . . .

UFOs.

Many believe that the Bermuda Triangle is heavily traveled by UFOs, and that these extraterrestrials abduct the travelers. This seemed to be a very popular theory, and Russell could see why they saved it for last. But seriously, *aliens in Fairfield?*

According to some of the stories Russell had heard from his schoolmates, the idea may not be all that farfetched. But for the moment, something that fantastic seemed the most unlikely to be proven.

Russell's head spun with possibilities.

Finally, Mr. Barker snapped him out of it.

"So, what do you think, Russell? Was there anything on the tape you thought might explain how our things vanished?"

Russell shook his head.

"Those disappearances just seem so . . . big. They make the Fairfield Triangle look unimportant by comparison."

"Then you should study our Triangle's history," remarked Brenna, bringing Russell a soda from the kitchen. "Lots of things have gone on there that I bet you don't know about. Dad could show you."

Russell turned to Mr. Barker, who sat in his easy chair, rubbing his chin.

"Let's go up to my studio, Russell," he said.

Russell jumped to his feet and, along with Brenna, followed Mr. Barker up the stairs.

Russell had been to the Barker's house twice before. Once for the girls' eighth birthday party, another to mow Mr. Barker's lawn for him when he broke his foot while hiking Crier Mountain.

He had never been in Mr. Barker's studio.

Mr. Barker led them up the stairs to a closed room at the end of the hall. Just before they entered, the doorbell rang.

"I bet that's your dad, Russell," remarked Mr. Barker.

Russell couldn't hide the disappointment on

his face. He'd heard stories about the studio and had really wanted to see it.

Then Mr. Barker said, "Why don't you two go on in. Brenna can show you the notes I've collected on the Triangle. I've got some questions to ask your dad, anyway."

As Mr. Barker left them, Brenna opened the door and they stepped inside.

Russell's jaw dropped to the floor.

It looked like a miniature Disneyland, a shrunken Smithsonian, and a reduced Fairfield Library collected all in one room. There were shelves of books, hardcover and paperback, with titles ranging from the fictional *Frankenstein* to the nonfiction UFO books by Jacques Vallee. They lined huge wooden shelves that practically touched the ceiling. And the ceiling! There were painted illustrations depicting a number of story-telling scenes.

"A few of the stories from *Mythology*, the book on Greek myths," explained Brenna, noticing Russell gaze upwards. "Dad loves that book."

Russell's eyes took in the rest of the room's candy. There were models displayed in every nook—a plesiosaur, a yeti, even a Testor model of the Roswell UFO.

Then, over in one set-off corner, were pictures hanging from a makeshift rack with the word "preliminary" marked above them. Russell recognized some of the places in the photos right away: the Starlight Drive-In, the Museum of Science and Natural History, the Fairfield Express Depot . . .

"Those are test shots for his new book," said Brenna. "He took them while on a drive through Fairfield. But the Triangle was his first big shoot. Addy, Crystal—we need the computer."

The names jarred Russell out of his daze. He hadn't even seen the two girls at the computer which sat on a desk wedged tightly between two of the larger shelf units.

"You're just in time, Brenna!" exclaimed Addy. "Maybe you can help me stop Crystal. She's *killing things* again!"

"Addy, you've got to stop taking these computer games so seriously," said Brenna, shaking her head. "C'mon, Crystal. Give it up."

"It's all yours," snickered Crystal. "My work's done here." She slowly lifted herself from the seat, leaving a robot from the game *Nexus* exploding wildly on the screen.

Brenna sat down, closed out the game, and

quickly called up some of her father's research files.

"Here we are. The Fairfield Triangle. The first thing he wanted to uncover in this investigation was exactly how many disappearances have been reported in the Triangle. Care to take a guess?"

Russell began to decline but then gave an answer.

"Fifty?"

"No. Way off. Almost three times that many. At least one hundred and thirty-three since the year 1872," Brenna announced.

"How'd he get that number?" Crystal asked.

"Many of them were reported to the police, and are now a matter of public record. Anyone can look them up. Dad got about one hundred and twenty of these from those records, the other incidents were given to him by locals," answered Brenna. She pulled more information up on the screen.

"Then he learned that the Triangle itself covers about five square miles," Brenna continued. "He did some map configurations and found out that the center of the thing is not in that field like most people believe, but deeper in the woods. Dad said he would have eventually trekked to the center if his equipment hadn't disappeared."

"Five square miles? That would put it right over some of the local roads," Russell realized.

"You bet. Some of the more interesting disappearances have happened on some of those same backways. In 1968, Jimmy Vanderburg, a local stock-car driver, vanished on Blood Creek Highway en route to a race. In 1974, four semitrucks were found deserted just off of Potter's Field. The drivers were never found. Then, of course, you've got the Mullinfield Marauders' disappearance."

"Oh, I've heard of that one. It's terrible, Russell. And it really makes you feel for Mullinfield," said Addy.

"What is it?" asked Russell.

"The Mullinfield Marauders were a biker gang that had a score to settle with the Fairfield Freebirds back in 1965. In a motorcycle convoy, the Marauders rode to Fairfield, arriving here late in the evening. They set up camp just outside of town, but unknown to them, it was right in the middle of the Fairfield Triangle. The gang sent three scouts into town to find out what the Freebirds were up to. When the scouts returned the next morning, they found the entire gang had vanished. Everything, right down to the last leather cap, was gone. None of the gang was ever heard from again."

Crystal couldn't contain herself anymore and exploded in laughter, snorting as she did so.

Addy shook her head at her disbelieving sister. "No respect for the vanished," she muttered.

Russell tuned them both out, carefully considering the information. He had entered the Fairfield Triangle that day thinking of it as nothing more than a local spook tale. Then he lost his kit. Now, in the last few moments, he'd heard enough information to help him formulate his next move.

"Do you want to hear more?" Brenna asked.

"No, I can't. My dad's probably waiting on me. Could you print out a copy of those notes for me?" Russell asked.

Brenna tensed up.

"I don't think I can," she said. "These are Dad's notes for his new book. I'm sure he wouldn't want them floating around in other people's hands."

"Please, I'm going to *need* them," Russell urged.

"Why? What are you going to do?" asked Brenna.

"The only thing I *can*. Return to the Fairfield Triangle."

6

Addy, Brenna, and Crystal met Russell at Brinkman's Art Supply the next morning. They found him testing various charcoal pencils over a rough scratch sheet.

"I knew he had an artist's soul," remarked Addy as the trio came up beside him.

"I'm no artist," muttered Russell, the tip of his tongue peeking through his lips, his eyes locked on the paper. "But I do know charcoal."

He stopped scratching on the sheet and handed the pencil to Old Mr. Brinkman.

"I'll take this one," said Russell.

"So are you returning to the Fairfield Triangle just to draw the place, or what?" asked Crystal.

"Nope. I lost my kit. So now I'm temporarily replacing it. This charcoal makes great fingerprint powder."

"Fingerprints?" asked Crystal. "What are you going to get fingerprints from out there? Tree bark? Grass blades?"

"Don't be obtuse. I'm hoping to collect a print or two from this," Russell said, pulling the baggied bottle cap from his pocket.

"Wow, Russell, you're almost at the bottom of this one," Crystal cracked.

Russell let her have her fun.

"I picked this up in the Triangle yesterday. My dad kept telling me it was a useless clue, and when I needed money for art supplies, I was inclined to believe him. It's a triple-winner. But when I got to the Quiki Mart counter to cash it in, I discovered this . . ."

Russell laid the bottlecap on the counter. It instantly began to move inside the baggie. Then it slid down the length of the counter and stuck to the metal cash register.

"Telekinesis?" gasped Addy.

"Magnetism," corrected Brenna.

Russell nodded his head.

"Something turned that bottlecap into one strong little magnet. Luckily, I never took it out of the baggie. I'm going to dust it for prints, and maybe we can find out who visited the area after your dad left. My bet is we'll also find some more of these refrigerator decorations, too."

Four bicycles raced to the outskirts of town, turning down the old dirt road where the mysterious field awaited them.

Russell had anticipated the mud, but neglected to warn the three sisters. Addy and Brenna slowed to a stop. Crystal rode on through, following Russell's lead as he coasted through the slop. He reached the grass at the end of the trail, surprised to see the mean sister slam on her brakes and stop beside him.

"Nice riding," he commented.

"Custom tires, just like yours," she replied. "I like to be prepared."

"Me, too," remarked Russell, getting off his bike and pulling his backpack off. He reached into it and pulled out a compass.

"What's that for?" Crystal asked. "Are you lost already, detective boy?"

"No, I'm running a test," he said.

"What kind of test?" Crystal pushed, trying to get an emotional response from the unemotional investigator.

"I'm attempting to determine any sizable magnetic readings from this area," Russell explained. "But my compass is only reading the magnetic north—the same place all compasses point. If a heavy magnetic presence hung in this area, I figured my readings might be a little . . . different."

"But they're not."

"No," he answered.

"Well that's a bust. *Hey Brenna!* Matlock here brought us to the Triangle for nothing," Crystal yelled as Brenna and Addy emerged from the trail, walking their bikes into the field.

"Remember, Russell," said Brenna. "This isn't really the center of the Triangle. Your readings may be totally different there."

"I'm not sold on that," said Russell. "Things have been disappearing all over the Triangle. What would make the center any different?"

"Wow, for a detective, you're seriously missing the chance to capitalize on an obvious metaphor," Addy cut in.

"Excuse me?" Russell asked, looking at her like she had just landed from Mars, speaking Pig Latin. "What are you talking about?"

"The Triangle. That's your problem," the

weird sister continued.

"And your point is . . ." Russell urged.

"You have a problem Now, how do you solve most problems?" Addy asked.

"I have *my* methods. What are *yours*?" Russell countered.

"You get to the *center of them*. Get it? The center of your problem? The center of the Triangle? To solve your problem, you must go to the center of the Triangle!" Addy finished.

"What? Well, that's crazy. I'm afraid that argument just isn't very convincing, Addy," Russell said.

"I think I know why he doesn't want to go there," Crystal smirked. "He's chicken. A regular Scooby-Doo mystery solver."

"I am *not* a Scooby Doo . . .," Russell started to defend himself, but Brenna jumped in.

"Russell, I just think it's worth a look. Dad believes the center has great importance! I think we would be making a sloppy case of it if we didn't check out that area."

A sloppy case. *Russell Drake would never be associated with those words.*

"Okay," he said. "Which way do we go from here?"

Brenna reached into her own backpack and pulled out her father's map of the area. She studied it for a second, then looked over the field.

"Over there," she said, pointing to where Russell and his father had heard the frightening noises.

Russell grimaced, remembering the earlier terror. He had felt something out there. Something . . . *horrible*. And it may still be in those woods, awaiting visitors.

"Let's go check it out," he said, and they headed for the edge of the trees.

7

The quartet slowly advanced into the woods as the daylight dimmed. The tree branches formed a dense black net overhead, shutting out the bright sky and keeping its hidden terrors trapped inside.

Russell led the group. He went cautiously, grasping thin trees to lower himself down the muddied hills left by the rain.

The girls followed him closely: Addy first, then Brenna. Crystal brought up the rear, looking over her shoulder every thirty seconds.

"It looks like it's getting even darker," whispered Addy.

Russell nodded. He couldn't *explain* their need to be as quiet as possible, but it seemed like a good idea. As the sunlight grew more scarce, they all quieted down.

It felt unnatural to Russell. The deeper into this *shadowplace* he ventured, the more dead it seemed to him. The trees showed more signs of rot. The sounds of the birds faded off in the distance. Every step Russell and the others took became increasingly loud. Their very breaths seemed to shatter the silence and alarm the unknown horrors that perhaps awaited them.

Each of them could feel it: the anticipation—the sparkling flame of fear that grew larger and burned brighter with every step they took. Each of them was primed to explode at the drop of a pin. They waited for that savage hammer to fall.

And it did.

Russell's foot kicked something into the air, sending it sliding loudly down the hill.

Addy screamed. Brenna jerked back, grabbing Crystal's arm. Crystal simply froze. She watched Russell with unblinking eyes.

He didn't move. For a moment, it looked as if every muscle in his body had been petrified, leaving his shell a cold memorial to the horror of being surprised.

"What is it?" Crystal asked, the first to catch her breath.

Russell finally moved. He lowered himself to the bottom of the hill, bent over, and picked up something.

"What is it?" Crystal repeated.

"A bottle," Russell answered, "a Loopy Cola bottle."

The girls all breathed sighs of relief, then climbed down the hill to join him. Russell still stared at the bottle in his hand as they reached him.

"Russell?" Brenna asked. "Are you okay?"

"It was a good idea, Brenna," he said. "Coming down here, I mean. We're definitely on the right track."

He pulled the metal cap from his pocket and placed it on top of the bottle. It seemed to fit perfectly.

"That doesn't mean anything," said Crystal. "Bottlecaps fit on bottles. That's what they do."

"You're right. But in this case, we're talking about one obscure bottle. Most bottles today are shorter and have a plastic lid. With this one, you have to use a bottle opener. Now add the facts: Loopy Cola is hard to find around here *and* these items were found relatively close to each other in such a deserted area. It's a perfectly safe assumption that this cap came from this bottle."

"So what are you saying? A litterbug stole our dad's equipment?" snapped Crystal.

"No, that's not it," Russell started, as he pulled the compass from his pocket and checked it. His mouth cracked open slightly. He held the compass up for the others to see.

The needle spun around and around, not stopping at all.

"What does that mean?" asked Addy. "Are we lost for good?"

"Let's hope not," choked Russell, feeling his blood rush from his brain.

Suddenly, the compass flew from Russell's hand and disappeared into a shadowy hole formed by the drooping trees.

No one moved. No one even breathed. No one except Addy, who began to hyperventilate.

The bottle in Russell's hand shook wildly until the metal cap freed itself and followed the compass into the woods.

Addy backed away just as her hair lifted over her head, her metal barrette pulling it forward. Too terrified to scream, she grabbed her hair, trying to keep it from being pulled out of her scalp.

Brenna and Crystal grabbed her and struggled to unlatch the barrette. Finally, it unsnapped and soared through the air into the darkness.

Other things took flight as well. Brenna's ring ripped straight off her finger. Two metal pens shot out of Russell's backpack, soaring like torpedoes through the air.

Then, somewhere in the shadowy hole, wood began to split. They could hear the branches crack—almost as if the trees were being pulled apart.

Then Russell saw the first beam of light— white light—just as he'd seen the day before. It beamed through the cross-thatched trees like a train speeding through a cave. The light tore through the woods, splintering and uprooting the trees as it came at them.

No one had time to scream.

In a blinding flash, the woods filled with the white light. Russell couldn't see, but he instinctively hit the dirt, rolling away from exploding terror. He went over the edge of a drop-off just as the earth exploded behind him. Pounds of mud showered down on him as he tumbled into a large puddle.

Slowly, Russell's vision returned. At that moment, something landed in the water beside him.

8

"Brenna!" Russell cried. "What is it?"

Brenna pulled her face from the mud, staring at Russell with wide-eyed confusion.

"It—it roared," she whispered.

Russell checked his memory. It *had* roared. An animal. A fierce beast had attacked them, and he couldn't see what had happened to Crystal and Addy.

Summoning his courage, Russell peeked out of the trench he had fallen into and saw something he couldn't believe.

A Jeep.

A Jeep Cherokee settled in the debris-filled muddy spot where the four of them had just been standing.

Brenna saw it too, and screamed.

"ADDY! CRYSTAL! ARE YOU OKAY?"

"We're over here," Crystal said in a low, shaken voice that came from the other side of the Jeep.

Russell and Brenna got to their feet and clambered up the hill. They stared at the truck, watching thin grey smoke drift from its hood, fenders, and tires. Its headlights flickered low, slowly dying.

They saw no one inside the wreck, but Russell heard Addy whimpering and saw both Crystal and her, lying face down on the ground like two soldiers trying to survive a shelling. Crystal had Addy's head covered, though it didn't keep her from shaking like a leaf.

"Are you guys all right?" Russell asked.

The two girls sat up, their hearts pounding in their throats.

"Is anybody in there?" asked Addy, still stunned.

As Russell helped the sisters up, Brenna looked through the window.

"There's no one in there at all," she said.

"No one at all?" Russell asked. "*Someone* had to have driven this thing through those trees. The engine was running. That's what roared!"

"And the lights?" Addy asked.

"The headlights," Crystal said dryly, "*very bright headlights*, that's what it had to have been." She seemed to be trying to convince herself rather than explain her theory to the rest of them.

"Hey! My ring!" exclaimed Brenna, grabbing hold of the jewelry stuck to the Jeep's hood. When she tried to yank it off, however, she couldn't. Then she steadied herself and pulled with all her strength, finally working it loose.

"Magnetized. Just like the bottlecap," Russell stated. Then he pulled the tire etching he'd made the day before from his pocket and compared it with the Jeep's tires. "They match," he said. "These tires made the tracks I found yesterday."

"You're saying this is the vehicle that came to the field after our father left?" Addy asked.

"It might be," Russell said.

"Then let's see whose it is!" snapped Crystal. "It may have registration or insurance papers or something in the car!"

As she made her way to the door, Russell stepped in front of her.

"We can't ruin the evidence," he said.

"*Ruin the evidence?* What are you talking

about? I'm *gathering* evidence! I'm going to find the rat who rolled this Jeep at me!" Crystal shouted.

"We have to call my dad in on this," said Russell. "We have to leave this to the professionals. They'll find our culprit."

Crystal gave him a look that said "this stinks," while Brenna continued to pull their belongings from the hood.

"No, Brenna, don't!" exclaimed Russell. "They need to see those things. This is going to be hard enough to believe already."

"I think we should go now," said Addy softly.

The three of them looked at her. She watched the woods, hugging herself to stay warm. One could tell she sensed *danger*.

"Please," she begged. "Let's go."

Then something stormed through the brush. They turned their heads to find the source of the snapping limbs. *Something* tore through the woods around them, crashing through trees like a hurtling meteor. Just as screams rose in their throats . . .

It stopped.

As more debris fell to the ground and settled,

the kids watched for the next movement, any burst of motion.

It never came.

Their eyes wide, their mouths open, no one could find the nerve to speak, until Russell finally managed to move his lips.

"Let's get out of here," he said.

9

Chaos broke out at Dwayne Barker's house.

He had been sitting in his chair going through his Fairfield Triangle notes, deciding whether or not to include the chapter in his book. Just as he sat back wondering if he should even continue the writing, the four kids stormed in, speaking at once, out of breath and seemingly out of their heads. A flurry of details pummeled Mr. Barker's brain. A visit to the center of the Triangle. A soda bottle. Magnificent lights. A Jeep smashing through the trees. After minutes of this yammering, he finally settled them down and got the full story.

"We'd better call the police," he said.

Mr. Barker related the story to the Sheriff, who made it his number-one priority, probably because of his son's involvement. Sheriff Drake took two of his deputies to the site with him. Within two hours of speaking to Mr. Barker, he gave the author a call. The kids were on the edge of their seats, waiting for Mr. Barker to hang up the phone and fill them in. Finally, the conversation ended.

Mr. Barker looked at the kids very solemnly and said, "Wade and Ted Grumlet."

The words plowed into Russell's head. He tried to shove them out, but they hung there and started making sense.

Wade and Ted Grumlet. The two biggest practical jokers/troublemakers in Fairfield. Two brothers who had never graduated from high school because they were suspended for more days than they were in class. They had been nothing but thorns in Fairfield's side ever since; Painting their smiling faces on the sides of police cars, running cows onto the field during half time at homecoming, and driving their old pickup the wrong way down Main Street during the Independence Day parade are just a few examples of their idea of fun.

"It seems that the boys traded up last week, bought themselves a used Jeep Cherokee," said Mr. Barker.

"So *they* did this?" Brenna asked in confusion.

"The Sheriff seems to think they're behind the whole thing. He even checked with Mr. Reynolds at the pharmacy, who said the Grumlets were in there on the day my equipment disappeared. That explains your bottlecap clue, Russell," explained Mr. Barker. "Anyway, your dad thinks they've gone on some kind of pranking spree."

"THAT WAS NO PRANK!" shouted Addy. "THAT WAS AN ATTEMPT ON OUR LIVES!"

Mr. Barker tried to calm her down. "Well, it's going to be over soon. They're scouring the woods for those two now. The Sheriff said if he can't find them there, he'll search the town. He knows where those Grumlet boys like to hang out."

Addy shook her head in disbelief, unable to swallow this answer to the mystery. Brenna rubbed her chin in deep thought over this new revelation. Crystal nodded, familiar with the Grumlets' past actions. To her, it seemed highly possible the two goons played a part in scaring them all.

Russell had questions.

"Did Dad say if he found a trail the Jeep might have taken to end up where it did?"

"He said he was searching, but it was starting to rain there," answered Mr. Barker.

"What about our items that were stuck to the Jeep. Did he see that they were magnetized?"

"He didn't find any items on the Jeep," answered Mr. Barker.

"I'm glad I pulled my favorite ring from there," muttered Brenna.

Russell kicked the facts around in his head, then came up with some facts of his own.

"Mr. Barker, in all good sense, I cannot believe the Grumlets are behind this," Russell said.

"I must admit," Mr. Barker replied, "it doesn't sound like their usual kind of stunt."

"No, it doesn't," continued Russell. "The Grumlets love drawing attention to themselves. Before the Jeep appeared, however, this mystery would never have been associated with them. The case is too complex. The Grumlets aren't complex at all."

"You're right. It doesn't take a couple of geniuses to mow the word 'Stinky' into the

Mayor's lawn," Mr. Barker agreed.

"Right. That's why I believe this case is worth further investigation," announced Russell.

Brenna, who had been deep in thought and only half-listening, looked up. So did the other sisters.

"Further investigation?" asked Mr. Barker. "I don't know. Everything that's happened has probably happened for a reason. Something just may not want me to write about the Fairfield Triangle."

"If you don't," said Russell, "I think, after all of this, someone else will."

The statement rang true. Once it leaked to the public that someone tried to write about the Fairfield Triangle and couldn't, someone else would realize what a great story that would make. Mr. Barker shuddered at the thought of losing such a feature.

"You know," the author smiled, "I still have all of my video equipment."

Within the next five minutes, Dwayne Barker decided to give the Triangle *further study*. Within fifteen minutes, the kids had talked him into letting them come along.

10

Sheriff Drake didn't like the idea.

Sure, he had searched the area up and down, finding a few oddities here and there, but nothing to get suspicious about. He believed the area to be relatively safe, but when Dwayne Barker told him his plans to camp in the heart of the Triangle for a night, and that Russell had begged to tag along, Sheriff Drake began to have his doubts.

Then he thought of how Russell had worked so hard on the case. In the end, in spite of his misgivings, he decided to let his son go with the author. He wanted to close the book on this mystery once and for all. And maybe, *probably*, the Sheriff would check up on them himself later in the evening.

The group of five journeyed into the woods,

returning to the very spot where the Jeep had crashed. Russell watched in amazement as the Barkers made quick work of the tent, putting it up in a matter of minutes. Brenna later told him that they'd been camping so many times, each family member could probably do his or her part blindfolded.

Then Mr. Barker set up his equipment. He decided to place the camera a good distance away from the tent where the audio would have a better chance of picking up suspicious noises from the woods rather than the group's conversations. He walked up the moist incline where the Jeep had emerged, and set up the camera on its tripod. Positioning a flat wooden sheet beside it, he placed his recorder on top of it. After twenty minutes worth of wiring and testing visuals and sound, he made his way back to the campsite.

Brenna and Addy were preparing dinner; a makeshift stew of potatoes, celery, and carrots to cook over the fire Crystal had made. Russell's feeling of uselessness subsided once everyone gathered around the fire to wait for dinner.

As the sun dropped almost out of sight, Russell decided to bring up their purpose for the trip.

"So what do you think our chances are of

getting something on tape, Mr. Barker?" he asked.

Cleaning his glasses with his shirttail, Mr. Barker answered with a smile. "I don't know. If your father's theory holds up, we won't get much of anything. The Grumlets have probably been scared away from this area by now."

"Is that what you believe?" Russell asked.

Mr. Barker sighed slightly. "You know, I've seen a lot of amazing things in my life. I've been in the center of mysteries that would make this one pale in comparison; anomalies that are supposedly so fantastic, solving them would drive a man mad. But I have seen many of these mysteries solved. And all too often, they are proven to be hoaxes. Never discount the dull answers."

"So you believe the Fairfield Triangle is a hoax?" Russell asked.

"I might have," responded Mr. Barker, "if I hadn't experienced it for myself. When my equipment disappeared, I felt something out there—a presence much more powerful than any Grumlet."

"What do you think it is?" asked Russell.

"Until we can obtain evidence," said Mr. Barker. "It's a mystery."

11

"*I* believe the Grumlets *are* behind it," Crystal remarked.

Russell knew she felt that way. Fantastic or illogical theories exceeded her range of belief. Addy, on the other hand, looked appalled.

"How can you buy into a silly explanation like that?" she asked.

Crystal glanced at her and smiled. The mean Barker sister *liked* being challenged.

"The Grumlet theory covers all the bases," she said. "The Grumlets have always had a law-breaking reputation. With the exception of their personal battle with the Mayor, all of their pranks have involved prominent happenings in Fairfield at the time."

The stew had finished cooking, so Brenna pulled some bowls from her backpack and began spooning them full.

"So what's your point?" Brenna asked.

"Dad's book was prominently featured in the paper last week. The Grumlets haven't pulled a big stunt in a while, and when they saw Dad's story in the paper, their wheels started turning. Dad even mentioned in the article that his first investigation would be of the Fairfield Triangle," Crystal explained.

"That's true," said Mr. Barker. "But I never said *when* I would be documenting the area."

"That wouldn't matter to those goons. If they wanted to pull their prank right, they would watch the Triangle night and day. Then, as soon as your back was turned, Dad, they'd 'make something disappear,' like your camera equipment."

Addy had major problems with this explanation.

"Why would they do something like that?" she asked. "It's a little behind-the-scenes for them. It's not the grandstand kind of stunt those two are used to pulling."

Crystal tried to take a bite of stew, decided it was too hot, and continued explaining.

"Don't you see? This would be huge for them.

If they made Dad believe things really disappeared in the Triangle, he'd write about it in his book. Suddenly, the Fairfield Triangle would get visitors galore, tourists from all over the country. The Grumlets may have even planned a souvenir business on the side."

Russell had remained silent, listening to the entire story before pushing her further.

"It's a sound theory," he said, "except for two things. How did the Jeep get into the woods, and what magnetized it?"

Crystal had been waiting for Russell to speak up. With a sly grin, she took on the questions.

"First off, I believe having the Jeep come after us wasn't part of their plan at all. It was an attempt to scare us away. Second, you're talking about a couple of guys who supposedly stole the Mayor's old Volvo and mailed it to him in small boxes for over a year. If they wanted to set up a base in the woods and not leave any tracks, they could've taken that Jeep apart and rebuilt it there. Then there's the magnetism. I think that, too, was a fluke. Just before the Jeep rolled at us, I believe it was struck by lightning."

"WHAT?" Brenna asked.

"That's my theory," said Crystal.

"Crystal, it's highly unlikely that a bolt of lightning struck and *magnetized* that Jeep," said Mr. Barker.

"Not to mention, the idea's completely out in left field," said Brenna.

"Oh yeah, super brain? What's your great take on the mystery?" asked Crystal.

"I've got one," said Brenna. "And I don't even have to manipulate the forces of Mother Nature to make my theory work."

Everyone continued to eat, anxiously awaiting Brenna's explanation.

12

Nighttime had overtaken the sky. The fire crackled and popped, illuminating four anxious faces as they waited for Brenna to speak.

"To me, the key to this whole thing seems to revolve around the magnetism," she said. "That's the biggest clue we have."

She looked over at Russell who nodded in agreement.

"What do you think causes the magnetism, Brenna?" Mr. Barker asked.

Russell could tell that the Barkers did this sort of thing all the time. Discussing theories on fantastic phenomena came naturally to all of them.

"In what I've read on the subject, many magnetic anomalies are attributed to large iron ore deposits under the area's surface. That might be the case here," she said.

"If that were so, wouldn't this be a mining town?" asked Russell, liking the idea, but needing more to chew on.

"Difficult to say," Mr. Barker cut in. "One concentrated lump under the earth could go undiscovered for a few lifetimes. Of course, I'm no expert on the subject . . ."

"But it *is* a possible answer," interjected Brenna, "that would not only explain why certain things become magnetized in this area, but it might also give a reason for the constant rains. It's been theorized that sizable magnetic anomaly could cause an atmospheric disturbance."

"Stop talking through your nose, Poindexter," remarked Crystal. "You said your theory didn't bend any of nature's rules. These magnetic anomalies sound like a desperate stab in the dark, if you ask me."

"It might explain the magnetic attraction and the rain storms," said Russell, "but what about the disappearances?"

"That's where I tend to agree with my sister." Brenna grimaced and glanced coldly at Crystal. "The disappearances in the area are of a human nature. I'm sure that if we looked at each case one at a time, we could find legitimate reasons for the disappearances."

"Really?" asked Addy in a nonbelieving tone. "Then what about Jimmy Vanderburg, the stock car driver? He disappeared on his way to that big race!"

"Yeah," Brenna sarcastically replied. "The big race. A lot of people say Jimmy was tired of racing and often claimed he'd like to just *disappear* somewhere."

"Well, what about those deserted semi-trucks?" Addy continued.

"Did you ever hear what those trucks were carrying? Smuggled fur coats! No wonder the drivers *mysteriously vanished*."

"What about the missing Mullinfield Marauders?" Addy pushed.

"They were a motorcycle gang. Nomads of the road. 'Nuff said," answered Brenna.

One could look at Addy's face and see the desperate search going on inside her head.

"And Dad's equipment?" Addy asked, hoping the question would be her saving grace.

"Wade and Ted Grumlet," Brenna said solemnly.

Addy shook her head in denial. These

weren't the answers she wanted to hear.

"Addy?" asked Mr. Barker. "Are you okay?"

"I just can't believe these are the answers," Addy said to him.

"Well, what do *you* believe?" Mr. Barker asked her.

This should be interesting, thought Russell.

13

Addy had finished her stew and set the empty bowl down at her side.

"I think Crystal and Brenna have very good explanations," she said, "but I believe their solutions just seem too . . . coincidental. I prefer one answer that covers all the bases."

"And what would that be?" asked Brenna.

"I believe the Fairfield Triangle is visited by aliens on a regular basis."

Crystal snorted a laugh.

Brenna tried to take her sister seriously, but could not keep a snicker from slipping out.

Russell and Mr. Barker looked at each other, bracing themselves for a wild explanation.

"Why would aliens visit this worthless chunk of land?" Crystal chortled.

Addy stiffened her nerves, determined not

to overreact.

"Why do aliens visit anywhere? The aliens simply use this area as a pick-up zone, abducting wandering humans and snatching their belongings every now and then to examine," explained Addy.

"What led you to come up with this theory?" asked Mr. Barker.

"Like I said, it answers everything very simply. The bright lights we saw—those came from the UFO or maybe one of its smaller scouts. Alien technology may rely heavily on magnetism, which would explain all of the magnetized objects we found. Abductions and samplings would explain every disappearance, Dad. Every one. No crazy magnetic anomalies. No improbable practical jokes. Just one simple, all-encompassing answer."

"What do you think, Russell?" Brenna asked.

Russell set his bowl down and cleared his throat.

"I think alien visitation is as legitimate a theory as anything else," he said. "All three solutions to the mystery are well-founded, and at this point, any of them could be true. For me, there just isn't enough information to make a deduction."

"I can't believe young Barnaby Jones here doesn't have *some* take on this case," Crystal said snidely. "Go with your gut feeling, man."

"I don't go by *feelings*. I weigh evidence. Right now, there just isn't enough of it," Russell stated.

"So when will there be enough evidence?" asked Addy. "This may be all you get."

"I'm not leaving the Fairfield Triangle until I retrieve my kit. And it looks like in order to do that, I'll have to solve its mystery. And when I solve it, I'll need proof to back up my answer," announced Russell.

"Well, if something does happen out there," said Mr. Barker, "we'll get proof. I've brought a dozen tapes, and—"

Without warning, a thunderous crash erupted just beyond the campsite. The five campers looked to the woods, their eyes searching for any oncoming invader.

Then Mr. Barker saw it.

14

"MY VIDEO CAMERA!" he exclaimed, jumping to his feet.

Russell peered into the woods, seeking the cause of Mr. Barker's anguish. Then he saw that the video setup had fallen over, probably a victim of the evening breeze or a small night animal. Still, with equipment that expensive, Russell could see why Mr. Barker would be so upset.

As her father stormed into the woods to check the setup, Brenna pressed her hand firmly against her heart.

"Whoa, that scared me," she said. "I thought it was . . ."

"An alien?" asked Addy.

"No!" answered Brenna.

"The Grumlets?" asked Crystal.

"No. Bigfoot. I thought it was Bigfoot. I've always been spooked by the Sasquatch."

"For me it was always Spring Heel Jack," Russell joined in, in an attempt to assimilate into the sisters' world of legendary myths.

"IT'S OKAY," Mr. Barker spoke loudly back to them. "She's up and running again."

He had just started back for the campsite, when suddenly a brilliant flash of light overtook him!

For an instant, the kids could see nothing but a white burst of illumination, almost as if the sun had landed in front of them.

Then the light vanished.

And so did Mr. Barker.

15

Addy didn't stop screaming for several minutes, exclaiming, "The aliens have taken Daddy! The aliens have taken Daddy!" Crystal finally settled her down, giving Russell a few precious seconds to grip reality and come up with their next move.

After the light disappeared, he had scoured the dark woods searching for Mr. Barker and any kind of movement. But there was only the red light of the video camera, fallen over again, but still recording.

On instinct, he ran to the camera, grabbed it, and brought it back to the tent. As Brenna called into the woods for her father, Russell rewound the tape, then hooked the camera up to a small battery-operated television Mr. Barker had brought with them. He felt sweat coat his palms as he hit the play button.

Brenna, meanwhile, didn't give up for several minutes. She couldn't bring herself to leave the light of the campfire, but she remained vigilant until Russell called to her.

"Brenna! Come here! It's all on tape! You've *got* to see this!" he cried.

Russell's call echoed in her head for a moment before she could tear herself away.

"Russell, we've got to get some help!" she sobbed, walking back to the tent.

"We will," he said. "But this . . . this is important."

Crystal left Addy's side, walked over to Russell, and pushed him off his log. He fell on his back, and before he could get up, he felt a fist press hard under his chin.

"LISTEN, SHERLOCK. OUR DAD'S MISSING! WE DON'T CARE WHAT'S ON THE STUPID TAPE. WE'VE GOT TO GET SOME HELP AND FIND HIM!" Crystal snarled.

Russell could hardly breathe, but managed to grunt the words, "Just look."

The tape had already started playing. The monitor showed the dense tree brush it had been pointing at after Mr. Barker set it back up.

Suddenly, the camera jerked and the image went into motion as the camcorder fell to the ground. When it landed, Mr. Barker came into view. One of the video cords had been wrapped around his foot.

Suddenly, the light appeared.

From this angle, they could see it plainly—swirling gases creating a funnel out of the air—a vortex, much like the Vile Vortices mentioned in the Bermuda Triangle tape. The light danced out of it as if it were a hole and someone shined a spotlight out from the other side.

Then something came out of it. Something weird. It wrapped itself around Mr. Barker and pulled him into the funnel. As soon as it fully engulfed him, the light and the swirling mist disappeared, leaving the kids screaming in the background and running up into the frame.

"What . . ." gasped Crystal. "What was that?"

Addy moved slowly over to the monitor, too scared out of her mind to watch. But she had to know.

Russell replayed it, and they watched it again.

"It looks like some kind of vortex," said Russell, glancing at Brenna for her opinion. She gave none but kept watching.

When the thing appeared out of the funnel, Addy choked on her scream, her muscles locking in terror.

Crystal watched in amazement.

"Tentacles. They look like tentacles," she said. "White tentacles, but practically transparent."

They watched the ropy arms of the unknown assailant wrap themselves around Mr. Barker. He didn't scream in pain. His face opened in total shock, and the look stayed there until the thing pulled him into the spinning funnel.

They all watched the tape one more time, committing every frame to memory. Then Russell pressed stop and yanked the tape from the recorder.

"This is proof," he said. "Hard evidence. When we go back for help, they're not going to believe us when we tell them what we saw. But when we play this tape, we'll have more help than we could wish for."

Brenna picked Russell's backpack off the ground.

"Then toss it in here," she said, "and let's go find help."

16

They started out, leaving the campsite behind them as they pointed their flashlights on the trail. The quartet moved quickly—though the girls occasionally looked back in hopes of seeing their father.

After climbing their fourth steep hill, Russell counted it as one too many.

"We must be going the wrong way," he said. "I don't remember coming down this many inclines."

"There was only one trail," said Brenna. "We're following the only one out of here. Let's keep moving."

Twenty minutes later, they were still in the woods.

"Okay. Let's admit it now," said Russell.

"We're lost."

Addy came up beside him and patted the tree he stood beside.

"I remember this tree from our walk down to the campsite. It has ugly knots in it that reminded me of a face. We're definitely on the right trail." She took some chalk out of her backpack and marked an "X" on the tree. "Just in case we lose the trail. We'll know we're on the right track if we come back to this marker."

No one argued against the idea. They trudged forward, up hill after hill, and in fifteen minutes came to a tree marked with an "X."

"What's going on?" asked Crystal almost ready to give up.

Russell shined his flashlight on the tree. The gnarled face of a crying man looked back at him.

They all screamed.

"No. No, this is it," said Addy. "This is the same tree. It's the exact same mark I made a while ago."

"Then we're walking around in circles," gasped Brenna, her hopes for getting help diminishing.

"We can't be," said Russell. "We've been walking uphill the whole time. We didn't change direction once!"

"Then what's happening?" Crystal snapped. "Can we not get out? Are we trapped here?"

"It's like the woods are changing," said Addy. "They're keeping us from finding a way out."

Russell shined his light over to his left. The ground seemed clear enough to walk on.

"Let's go this way," he said, storming off in the new direction.

The girls followed. In a few short minutes they ended up back at the tree.

"THIS IS INSANE!" Crystal cried.

"Russell, I don't think we can get out of here," said Brenna. "I think Addy's right. Something's keeping us inside the woods."

Russell turned around slowly, letting his light point in every direction.

"How is this possible?" he asked.

Then his light hit something shiny, resulting in a flash that startled him. He yelled and dropped the flashlight.

"WHAT IS IT?" cried Brenna. "WHAT DID YOU SEE?"

Russell's shaky hand picked up the light and pointed it back toward the flash. The object didn't move. It merely glimmered in the glow of the flashlight. Russell moved closer to get a better look.

"Some kind of metal or plastic," he muttered, slightly irritated with himself for being so jumpy—though he had every right to be. He picked up the find.

"What is it?" Brenna repeated.

"It's . . . a helmet," Russell said, holding it up to his face. "A red racing helmet."

He walked back over to the sisters.

"Brenna," he asked, "you would know. What was Jimmy Vanderburg's racing number?"

"Thirty-three," she said. "Why? What's that one?"

Russell spun the helmet around so they could see.

"Thirty-three," he said.

The girls stood in silence, staring at one of the most important finds in Fairfield's history.

"That's not all," Russell said. "This is the first item in a long trail of junk. It goes over the edge of that hill."

The group stared at each other for a moment, then walked over to the small ridge, never once questioning whether they should or not.

When they reached the edge, Russell shined his light on the other side. The girls also pointed their flashlights over the tiny valley awaiting them on the other side.

What they saw took their breaths away.

<u>17</u>

"It's here," muttered Brenna. "It's all here."

Flooding the dark crater with light, the answers to a hundred mysteries lay spread before them.

A junkyard. A massive junkyard full of lost items.

Cars, trucks, bicycles, and all kinds of other miscellaneous objects were scattered over the opening, piled high to fill the large hole practically halfway.

Brenna realized the origin of the items before anyone else. She spied Jimmy Vanderburg's red and yellow stock car crammed between a semi-trailer and a half dozen motorcycles. Then she noticed the inscription on one of the motorcycles: The Mullinfield Marauders.

"I can't believe it," she continued. "These are

all the things lost to the Triangle! We've found them!"

The realization electrified Russell, and he swept his flashlight over every crack and crevice of the hidden junkyard.

He stopped when he saw his light reflect off of a small object partially hidden under one of the cars—something made of glass.

"I'm going down there," Russell said, already on his way before any of the girls could say a word.

He lowered himself carefully, stepping around and over jutting metal scraps and the remaining shards of windows and windshields.

Russell reached the car that hid his quarry and began feeling around beneath it for his prize. His hand touched smooth rounded glass. Straining further, he wrapped his hand around a wooden handle and pulled out the object. His cherished magnifying glass shined in the moonlight.

"WHAT DID YOU FIND?" asked Brenna.

"MY MAGNIFYING GLASS!" he cried. "The rest of my kit has to be down here, too." He flashed the light over the heap, searching for the remaining pieces of his missing treasure.

"WE DON'T HAVE TIME TO WASTE LOOKING THROUGH THAT JUNK! WE'VE GOT TO FIND

OUR WAY OUT OF HERE!" yelled Crystal, pacing back and forth at the top of the hill.

"I HAVE TO KEEP LOOKING!" Russell shouted back. "NO ONE'S EVER FOUND THIS PLACE BEFORE! IF WE LEAVE, WE MAY NEVER FIND IT AGAIN! I HAVE TO FIND THE REST OF MY KIT WHILE I'M STILL HERE!"

"RUSSELL! LOOK OUT!" screamed Addy.

Russell spun around and saw the pile of cars behind him teeter and slide forward. Then the entire stack came crashing down. Russell bolted, leaping far enough out of the way to avoid the crashing tower. He landed at the hood of a car that stood on its front end, just as the cars hit the ground and rolled over.

The young detective sat pressed against the up-ended car, breathlessly gazing at the dust-kicking carnage that settled before him. He felt something dropping on his head.

He looked up and saw a human skeleton hanging over the car's dashboard. The reverberations from the falling cars had loosened tiny bits of debris from the wreckage, and they were dropping from inside the car and bouncing off of Russell's head. Then the skeleton slid and fell from the seat. He didn't have a chance to yell.

"RUSSELL! RUSSELL! ARE YOU OKAY?" shouted Brenna.

Russell wrestled with the dirty bones that had dropped on top of him. He threw them to the ground and frantically checked himself to make sure there weren't any more skeleton pieces hanging from him.

"THERE AREN'T ONLY CARS AND TRUCKS DOWN HERE!" Russell screamed. **"THERE ARE ALSO *THE DRIVERS* OF THE CARS AND TRUCKS!"**

"You mean . . . there are *people* down there?" asked a sickened Addy.

Russell grabbed his flashlight from the ground, shined it over at the red and yellow stock car, and noticed a drooping skeleton that he'd missed before.

"You could come speak to Jimmy Vanderburg," he said, "but I can't promise he'll talk back."

"RUSSELL, GET OUT OF THERE! WE'LL MARK OUR TRAIL HERE AND COME BACK AND GET YOUR KIT! WE HAVE TO SAVE DAD!" cried Brenna.

Russell retrieved the magnifying glass he'd let slip to the ground. He shined the flashlight over the junkyard one last time.

No matter how badly he wanted his kit back, Mr. Barker came first.

"I'm coming up," said Russell.

When he dug his foot into the side of the hill to climb up, he felt something odd. The ground seemed to move underneath him. It oozed beneath his foot.

Russell gasped and looked down.

He had stepped on something alive. *Large* and alive. It lifted itself from the ground, and all four kids screamed.

18

Russell jumped back from the moving thing and landed on his back, forcing the wind from his lungs.

The thing reared up, exhibiting its form to the horrified eyes of Addy, Crystal, Brenna, and Russell. It had been camouflaged—its color the same as the dirt-covered hill. To Russell, its skin seemed almost gelatinous, somewhat like a water balloon. He felt it again as it wrapped around his leg. In that instant, he remembered the tentacles on the videotape.

Like a chameleon, the creature adapted almost seamlessly to the color of its surroundings. Russell couldn't even see the tentacle to slap at it.

Then he saw Addy and Brenna roll down the hill, almost as if they were being pulled.

"NOOOOO!" Addy screamed, clawing her fingers in the dirt. The thing *did* have them.

"LET THEM GO!" Crystal shouted, and with remarkable strength, she lifted a large rock from the ground and launched it at the creature.

It struck the thing right in the center, the impact resulting in a fantastic burst of light that sprayed over the junkyard and showered down like liquid. A high-pitched shriek erupted from the creature as its grip on the kids loosened. Russell, Brenna, and Addy made a break for it, scattering into the junkyard and away from the recovering creature.

Crystal ran along the outside edge of the debris-filled crater, calling to her sisters as she darted through the trees.

"ADDY! BRENNA! WAIT FOR ME!" she screamed, just as the air in front of her opened up, exposing a winding vortex of swirling gases.

She stopped in her tracks. From out of the open hole in space, the squirming white tentacles wriggled out and reached for Crystal, who immediately jumped behind a tree.

The snaking tendrils roped around the tree's trunk *and* Crystal. She choked out a scream as the creature pulled. The base of the tree cracked and splintered.

Just as the air was almost squeezed from her lungs, the tree snapped back, and the creature relieved some of the pressure as if to get a better grip. In a flash, Crystal's hand scooped up one of the wood shards and drove it into the constricting tentacle.

The creature screamed and loosened its grip, allowing Crystal to run off, gasping for air, but not stopping to rest.

Addy and Brenna heard the awful cry of pain and stopped.

"Crystal?" Brenna breathed, then, **"CRYSTAL!"**

Their eyes searched the woods for their missing sister.

"Brenna," Addy whispered. "I don't see her . . ."

Suddenly, a bright light flashed above their heads, and one of the large creatures crashed to the ground. The girls shot out of the way as its slimy arms instantly reached for the two escapees.

"OVER THE CARS!" Brenna cried, clambering up the side of Jed Faulkner's missing '76 Pinto. Addy followed, climbing just out of the tentacles' reach.

As she moved over the cars, Addy got a good look at the thing chasing them before it had a chance to camouflage itself.

It had a thin milky-white coating, stretched slightly tighter than a jellyfish's covering. Its shape looked close to a bowling pin's, though fatter at the bottom and with a rounder head. Through the creature's translucent skin, Addy could see what appeared to be a network of veins sending bright, illuminating impulses throughout the creature's body.

The tentacles jutted from its stomach, winding around themselves like thick spaghetti noodles with minds of their own. It had two large, empty, grey eyes glossed over by a thick, clear membrane.

Below the eyes moved a grotesque mouth, very similar to a fly's. It sucked the air, presumably searching for something juicy to eat.

Folded behind the creature were long curtains of flesh. They dragged on the ground like extra-heavy elephant ears, and Addy blessed them for they hindered the creature enough for them to get away.

"KEEP CLIMBING!" Brenna screamed in Addy's ear. **"ITS ARMS CAN STILL GET US!"**

As the duo crawled over the heap of rusted Mullinfield Marauder choppers, the tendrils caught up with them—wrapping around Addy's legs! Before she could struggle, the creature's arm flashed with tiny bursts of light, making Addy cry out in agony.

"**ADDY!**" Brenna screamed, losing her footing. She slid on the pile of motorcycles, grabbing the first thing she could to halt her descent. Her hands clung to the bony neck of a skeletal Mullinfield Marauder. Its spiked motorcycle helmet, still fitted to the top of the skull, came dangerously close to poking Brenna in the eye as she pulled herself up.

"**LET HER GO!**" Brenna cried as she brought the spiked helmet over her head and thrust it into the creature's arm.

The thing shrieked, let go, and reared in pain, giving Brenna the second she needed to grab Addy, who did very little to help herself as her body twitched with painful spasms. Brenna desperately struggled to pull her from harm's way.

The creature charged again. Just as Brenna gave up hope, another pair of hands locked around Addy's wrist and helped pull her to safety.

"CRYSTAL!" Brenna exclaimed, shocked to see her sister alive and well.

"What happened to Addy?" Crystal asked, pulling her shaking sister over the top of the motorcycle pile to a safe alcove.

"That thing stung her, I think," answered Brenna. "It's full of some kind of electrical charge."

"I guess I got lucky," Crystal said. "One of them grabbed me, but I got away okay! Where's Russell?"

Just as the question left her lips, the pile of junk they were hiding behind moved. The sisters could see the translucent tendrils gripping the choppers and other car parts, pulling them out of the way to get to the three girls.

The creature broke through as the girls started to move. The stringy arms slithered in, ready to squeeze the life out of the Barker sisters.

Suddenly a pile of cars next to the creature lurched, moaned, and toppled over, crushing the creature beneath it. Light blasted from under the carnage, turning into neon drips that spattered over the surrounding scrap metal.

Crystal and Brenna closed their eyes,

avoiding the shower of gleaming goo.

"Wh-What is this stuff?" cringed Crystal.

"I think it's . . . blood," Brenna ventured. "Oh, I think I'm going to be sick."

As she lurched forward, another figure emerged through the floating dust of the fallen cars.

"IS EVERYBODY OKAY?" Russell shouted.

Brenna's constitution strengthened. Even Crystal smiled when she saw the young detective.

"ADDY'S BEEN HURT!" Crystal called over. "WE THINK THAT THING STUNG HER."

Russell came closer, jumping from car to car.

"How many were there?" he asked.

"Two, maybe three," Brenna replied. She kneeled over Addy, noticing the light perspiration that dotted her forehead. The spasms had subsided, but Addy's eyes stayed closed and her breathing shallow.

"Russell, we've got to find a way out of here, now! I think Addy's in serious trouble here!"

Russell looked at the tentacles convulsing under the heap of cars. He suddenly became furious with himself for not bringing a camera. He had thought the sisters would bring one.

They had thought he would. Now, with all of the evidence and proof lying before him—the very secrets of the Fairfield Triangle—he couldn't document it.

Crystal knew what he was thinking. She could see it on his face.

"Don't sweat it, Magnum P.I.," Crystal said. "I think you've got enough evidence!"

A fuse blew in Russell's head.

"That's right! The tape! I haven't checked on it! It could've been damaged in one of my falls!"

Russell yanked off his backpack, ripped it open, and pulled out the tape. It remained in pristine condition.

"*Whew.* As long as we have this," he said, "something will come from this disaster."

A vortex appeared behind him. Before Russell knew it, the already familiar tentacles had coiled around his waist and pulled him through the spinning hole.

19

Wind rushed around him.

Rays of light cut into his eyes, forcing them shut.

The creature dragged Russell blindly *through* the vortex to *its* side. The turbulence bounced the young detective up and down, and he felt . . . *tingles.* Tiny surges of electricity hummed against his skin, sending shivers through his body. They exuded from the thing—whatever it was. *Phantoms,* Russell thought. Things that blink in and out in the dead of night and snatch people from their homes and streets and cars. Although they don't match the classic image of the shadowy phantom, creeping along alleys and pulling victims into the dark, these were a hideous new breed. Once *they* have you, you're never found again.

They leave no evidence at all.

The phantom continued its trip through the windy funnel, pulling Russell over the bumpy currents until finally, the gusts disappeared and the rushing white wind turned into a rippling vibrant blue.

Russell's muscles relaxed. He let the creature drag him through what felt like an ocean of air. Heavy, tingling waves swept over him, giving him the constant sensation of shivering in the cold.

But this place felt warm, a total contrast to the cool blue atmosphere. The pounding drift made his head ache. Drowsiness set in.

He looked around and saw vortices opening and closing everywhere, allowing creatures to exit from and enter into the grand realm.

Russell couldn't see where the phantom was carrying him. They approached a large, white, honeycombed crystal floating freely in the vast blue.

The phantom swooped down, revealing its drooping backskin to be wings. It soared to the crystal's surface, hovered over one of the honeycombed holes, and dropped Russell into it. His backpack landed just outside the hole. It opened and spilled his possessions everywhere.

When he hit the bottom of the hole, he quickly got to his feet and attempted to crawl out. When he got to the top he screamed in horror.

In the next hole, sealed in by some spongy material, was a skeleton. It wore a hat on the top of its skull that read WADE.

Russell continued to scream, seeing a set of matching bones a few holes away. Its hat read TED.

The Grumlet brothers had become victims of the Fairfield Triangle. Russell didn't want to share the same fate.

As he scrambled further out of the hole, a phantom landed and sprayed a glowing foam over Russell. It kept him in the hole with its tentacles, knocking him back and forth so much that he couldn't keep his balance.

Russell couldn't bring himself to scream anymore, fearful of gulping some of the goo spewing from the creature's mouth. Soon, the entire hole brimmed with the glowing liquid, which quickly began to solidify. Only Russell's head stuck out from the top.

Then, like music to the young detective's ears, he heard another human voice. A familiar one.

"LEAVE ME ALONE! LET ME OUT OF HERE!"

Mr. Barker's voice!

The phantom above Russell's head unfolded its wings and lifted itself into the air. Now Russell could see Mr. Barker running over the sealed honeycombed landscape, chased by two other phantoms.

"MR. BARKER!" cried Russell. **"HELP ME!"**

Dwayne stopped in his tracks as he turned toward Russell. This gave the phantoms all the time in the world to overtake him. The two creatures on his tail lowered themselves, wriggled their snaky arms around Mr. Barker's leg and arm, then zapped him with an electrical pulse. He screamed in pain. When a third landed to join in on the torturing, Russell knew Mr. Barker didn't have much time.

20

Russell could feel his heart slamming against his chest, reverberating through his spongy cell. Panic had overcome him. He looked around for something, *anything*, to help him escape.

His eyes shot over to Wade, who offered no words of encouragement at all. Then Russell noticed something blue crawling all over Wade's skull. They were slightly smaller than ants, and without their bright-blue hue, Russell wouldn't have been able to see them at all.

Russell's eyes lowered to see a chain hanging around Wade's neck. From the chain, hung a pocketknife reading DRAKE on the side. Russell's pocketknife from his own investigation kit! That could only mean those two creeps had taken it! It hadn't "disappeared" in the Fairfield

Triangle after all!

Mr. Barker's screams snapped Russell back into reality. He looked in front of him. All of his stuff lay on the surface. The taped evidence still looked okay, but out of reach. His magnifying glass looked like the only thing within teeth-grabbing distance.

Russell stretched for it and noticed hundreds of the small blue things magnified through the glass. They were all moving in his direction.

Russell suddenly had a horrible thought. He was food. Food for the little blue "mites." The fates of Wade and Ted Grumlet then dawned on him, and he started struggling like mad to get free.

The solution that trapped him was hardening quickly. It already seemed impossible to move, but Russell strained. Finally he felt his arm moving somewhat easier. With every bit of his remaining strength, he pulled his left arm out.

After that, he couldn't budge. Every limb became completely immobile. He tried to dig himself out, but he couldn't rip into the substance. He needed something sharper.

The pocketknife. Reaching over as far as he

could, he came up two inches short of pulling the chain from around Wade's neck. He stretched again, hooked two fingers under Wade's top row of teeth, then pulled the skeleton his way.

Grabbing the pocketknife, he opened it with one hand (a trick he taught himself in case of capture someday), then started ripping into the encasing.

He looked up and saw the phantoms hovering over an unconscious Mr. Barker. They hadn't noticed Russell yet. He kept digging, almost clearing away enough stuff so that he could move his other arm.

Suddenly he felt stinging sensations all over his body, tiny pinpricks that made him want to scream in pain. He could see the mites on him, and if he didn't get them off quickly, he'd end up like the Grumlets.

He continued to dig frantically, and finally pulled his other arm free. He braced his hands and heaved himself out of the gunk . . .

Just as the phantoms discovered him.

21

The phantoms lifted themselves into the air and moved Russell's way.

He had only seconds to run.

He scooped up the magnifying glass and videotape, and stuffed them into his backpack just as the phantoms closed in.

He completely ducked under the first attacker as it swooped in to grab him. The next landed in front of Russell, blocking his path to Mr. Barker. The third landed behind him.

As soon as he felt it touch the ground behind him, Russell moved. The thing hadn't expected the boy to move so fast, and accidentally locked onto its counterpart, stinging it at full power. The jolted phantom squealed and lifted itself into the air, circling in a fit of pain.

Russell took the chance and bolted over to

Mr. Barker. As soon as he got there, he noticed the tiny mites covering Mr. Barker's entire body. He tried to quickly sweep them off, but they seemed to be stuck there. Unless Russell could find a way to get them off, the tiny animals would eat him alive.

He needed water, or *a vacuum*.

The vortices. He had seen many, opening and closing as he came in. The wind force through one of them would probably be enough to pull the mites off of them.

Then he heard a screech and saw the first phantom coming his way.

Fueled by panic, Russell grabbed Mr. Barker and pulled him toward the edge of the crystal hunk. Looking out into the sweeping blue space, he saw vortices popping up everywhere, with phantoms flying into and out of them.

As the phantom approached, Russell knew he didn't have many choices.

The creature reached them, winding its arms into position to grab Russell and sting away.

With one mighty yank, Russell pulled Mr. Barker and himself over the side.

The creature followed.

As Russell and Mr. Barker fell slowly, Russell watched the phantom drop behind them.

It came closer.

Closer.

Russell could still feel the mites stinging him all over, saw the quivering mouth of the phantom chasing them, and hoped a vortex door might open soon.

It did.

A funnel appeared just to the right of them and Russell shifted his weight to carry them into it.

Once they hit the windy pocket, they were sucked through it like seeds through a straw, and Russell could only think of one word.

SAVED.

22

The rushing air bounced them around like ping pong balls. Without a phantom's aid, the ride became a rough, twisted punishment. Russell thought the two of them would surely be torn apart.

He did feel the stinging disappear about halfway through the ride and guessed that his plan had worked, even if it ended up thrashing them senseless.

Then suddenly, the light got brighter, the wind got even rougher, and Russell could see an opening at the end of the funnel.

He could see the actual nighttime sky.

Then the vortex spit them out, launching them into the air.

They landed on a muddy hill and rolled to the bottom where Russell lay for a second, staring upwards and taking in the view.

They were back in the woods. Back in the Fairfield Triangle. And his head pounded in pain.

"RUSSELL!" Brenna screamed, making him wince in pain. Then she saw her father. "DAD!"

Brenna and Crystal had been trying to find their way out of the Triangle, but with no luck. Every turn still looked the same. They were carrying Addy, who seemed to grow increasingly feverish.

The sisters had grown fearful that they might never find their way out—Addy wouldn't be saved, and they'd never get help to find their father and Russell. At that low point, Russell and Mr. Barker had fallen from the sky and landed on the hill in front of them.

"IS DAD ALL RIGHT?" cried Crystal, shouldering Addy's weight. "IS HE ALIVE?"

"I think he's been stung just like Addy," Brenna grimaced. "Even worse."

"How's Russell?" Crystal asked, moving closer.

Russell heard the question, sat up, and moaned. He held his thumping head in his hands, trying to keep it from exploding.

"I'm alive," he said.

"What happened? Where were you?" Brenna asked.

Russell shook his head.

"That would take some explaining," he said. "Did—did you find a way out of here?"

Brenna shook her head.

Russell got up slowly. Brenna helped him stand. He looked around at the woods and thought he might pass out.

The trees were blinking in and out. One second they were there, the next they were more scattered.

"I—I think I'm going to be sick," he said. "I'm seeing two different sets of woods here."

Confused, Brenna looked out into the woods herself.

"What do you see besides a dense area of trees?" she asked.

"A not-so-dense area of trees, with a path just over there," said Russell, pointing to a small trail over to his right.

The truth struck Brenna.

"Crystal and I can't see that path. Russell, you can see the way out of here! I don't know how, but you can. You've got to lead us out of here!"

Russell groaned. The task seemed too taxing for his pounding head. He helped Brenna carry her father and they led Crystal and Addy through the woods.

At the first turn they were about to take, Crystal screamed a warning about the wall of trees blocking their path. Russell walked the group right through them.

"Mirages," said Brenna. "We've been lost in a bunch of mirages."

Behind them, another vortex opened and two phantoms sprung out in hot pursuit.

"Go, GO, **GO!**" yelled Crystal, practically pushing Russell, Brenna, and her father, forward.

Russell saw the two creatures that were after them. These two acted more desperate than any of the others he had encountered. The other phantoms hadn't tried to fly in this world, but now these were spreading wings, lifting themselves into the air for a few seconds, then dropping to the ground. It looked almost like hopping.

Still, they were coming on pretty fast.

"RUSSELL! GET US OUT OF HERE!" Crystal screamed.

The pain surged through Russell's head as he led them through the false settings, darting around trees and rocks that the sisters would never see.

What's more, Russell realized his ability to see the real woods was fading. They had to get out of there fast.

More vortices opened, dropping more translucent creatures to join in the chase.

The surroundings were blinking in and out faster now. Russell began bumping into trees and tripping over rocks.

Crystal practically had her head in their backs, pushing them forward despite whatever obstacle stood before them.

Brenna tried not to look back. At last count there had to be twenty of the things after them, screeching and grasping. The electric tentacles swooped so closely, the kids felt their neck hairs rise.

Russell reached the guessing point. The different images seemed to strobe, and he knew if he didn't find a way out in the next few seconds, the phantoms would overtake them.

Then he saw the flashing blue light.

After that, his "extra" vision totally blinked out on him.

Wishing for the best, Russell led Brenna and Crystal through a smattering of trees, not knowing the real from the unreal. He plowed on, gambling against the light being a mirage or a vortex or a crack of lightning. He prayed for an exit.

"WE MADE IT!" Brenna cried. **"WE'RE OUT!"**

Russell opened his eyes.

They had come out in the open field, where three police cars awaited them. Their blue lights flashed like beacons, and Russell could see someone standing out in front of them.

His father, Sheriff Drake.

The kids pulled themselves toward the squad cars, and the Sheriff's deputies ran out to help them with the injured.

The Sheriff ran to his son and hugged him.

"What happened in there, Son?" he asked.

"You won't believe me," said Russell, "until you've seen the evidence!"

The phantoms stopped at the edge of the

woods, staring at the whirling lights and the quarry that escaped them. Then, one by one, they backed away, hesitant to attack the strange blue lights that shined differently from their own. There would be other chances, other meals to snatch up and feed to their young, the blue mites.

23

Static filled the television screen.

"Magnetized," said Russell. "Of all the stupid ways to lose the world's most important evidence. It had to be those vortices. Stupid, magnetized vortices."

"Don't worry, Russell," said Mr. Barker, resting on the couch. The ordeal had left him with a sprained arm and ankle. He was also covered with stings and had to administer a special ointment on them. "I believe you one hundred percent."

"But you don't even *remember* any of it. Neither does Addy. The fever those stings gave you wiped out the entire memory," Russell said.

"It doesn't sound like something I *want* to remember," said Mr. Barker, holding up his sprained arm. "But tell me, Russell, what do *you* think they were?"

"When I witness an odd chain of events, I try to compare them with an activity I'm familiar with. These creatures were fantastic, but I believe that what they were doing is a very common thing in our world. The phantoms, as I call them, would come through a vortex and snatch up someone to take back to their nest. They would leave their garbage in that big junkyard we found," explained Russell.

"What do you mean by nest?" asked Mr. Barker.

"Well, they would bring the unlucky person to their nest—the honeycombed structure we were in—and seal them up like they did me. Then they would ring the dinner bell for their kids."

"The *blue mites* you spoke of?" asked Mr. Barker.

"The blue mites. Schools of them would crawl over the meal and devour it, just as they did Wade and Ted Grumlet," said Russell.

"The Grumlets. What's your dad's official word on them?"

"Missing," answered Russell. "I don't think Dad places as much confidence in my story as you do. No evidence, you know."

Addy, Brenna, and Crystal came in from outside.

"Are you still watching that tape?" asked Crystal. "Give it up, Russell. The evidence is gone!"

"I was just discussing the case with your father in private, thank you," Russell replied snidely.

"Speaking of the case," said Brenna. "Did you ever figure out why you could see through those illusions in the forest and we couldn't?"

"I can only guess it's because of my exposure to their side of the vortex. Those phantoms projected the illusions somehow. I suspect being on their side conditioned me to their signal or channel or whatever it was they were using to throw up those mirages. I'm certain that's why my head was pounding." Russell answered.

"Hmmm . . .," said Brenna. "That's not bad. I'll put that theory in the book."

"What book?" asked Russell.

"My book," said Mr. Barker. "While I'm down and out, I decided to let Brenna continue my work for me."

"And me, too," Crystal nodded.

"You? You don't believe in any of that stuff," said Russell.

"Just because I'm a nay-sayer doesn't mean I'm blind," said Crystal.

"What about you, Addy? Are you helping, too?" asked Russell.

She shook her head.

"I've had enough fantastic phenomena for a while," she said. "The stuff is too *out there* for me."

"And you, Russell? What are you going to do with your fantastic story?" asked Mr. Barker.

"Nothing," Russell said. "I have no evidence. To me, with no proof to back up my case, the story isn't worth telling. Who knows? With all the attention this has brought to the Triangle, maybe someone else will collect that proof. Or maybe when all this excitement dies down, I'll make a *new* investigation kit and have another look at the area. Maybe *then* I'll gain my evidence. Regardless, this case remains open."

"Good show, Russell," said Mr. Barker. Then he yelped in pain.

"WHAT IS IT? WHAT'S WRONG?" asked Russell.

Mr. Barker rubbed his ankle, massaging it back to health.

"It's just my ankle wound," he said. "It stings every now and then. Small price to pay to live through something supposedly so *big*."

"Believe me," said Russell. "It happened."

Unseen by all of them, a small blue mite crawled from underneath Mr. Barker's bandages and rested comfortably after another full meal.

About the Authors

Marty M. Engle and **Johnny Ray Barnes Jr.**, graduates of the Art Institute of Atlanta, are the creators, writers, designers and illustrators of the **Strange Matter™** series and the **Strange Matter™ World Wide Web page.**

Their interests and expertise range from state of the art 3-D computer graphics and interactive multi-media, to books and scripts (television and motion picture).

Marty lives in La Jolla, California with his wife Jana and twin terror pets, Polly and Oreo.

Johnny Ray lives in Tierrasanta, California and spends every free moment with his fiancée, Meredith.

And now
an exciting preview
of the next

#19 Bigfoot, Big Trouble

by Marty M. Engle

1

Like everyone else, Dolly Hayes had heard the stories around the lake. And like everyone else, she tried to be polite, though she didn't believe a word.

She would nod and smile in the grocery store or the Pancake House, listening to the exaggerated tales of encounters with the beast—all the while wondering if her garbage cans were bear-proof.

Of course it was a bear.

Any other identification would be ridiculous. Impossible. She wasn't the type to believe in such things—things that only lived between the covers of the Weekly World News or some other shameless tabloid.

Over the last few weeks, more and more residents were claiming to have seen it—roaming the woods, picking through campsites, even running through yards. Maybe if she was younger, she would buy into the craziness, get excited about it. But not now. Her life was crazy enough. Between her weight, Gerald, and her check-out position at the Dollar General Store, she couldn't afford another worry.

Still, a bear was a pretty scary thought, particularly with her husband, Gerald, working nights at the plant.

He told her that if she ever saw or heard anything poking around outside the trailer, she should turn on all the lights and call the police. The last thing she should do is go outside and look around for the source of the noise. That, of course, was the thought that ran through her mind as she pulled on her wool overcoat and grabbed the flashlight off the kitchen counter.

The cold night wind whistled through the trees, blowing her long brown hair into tangles as she crept cautiously down the side of the trailer. The floodlights Gerald had installed last summer shined down through the misty rain like dim cones.

Of course, the lights didn't quite reach the metal trash cans in the backyard like Dolly had wanted. Whenever a noisy raccoon felt the need to search out a free meal, she wanted to be able to scare it off by simply flicking the light switch on and off from the comfort and safety of the kitchen. But no. Of course, he was always going to move the trash cans closer to the house.

She would have to go out there with a flashlight and shoo the things away by hand if she wanted to get any sleep. As experience had shown her time and again, those pests would keep at it all night, as loud as the Fourth of July.

She shined the flashlight in front of her like a weapon, sweeping it in arcs through the air and across the grass. A loud, sharp cry split the air.

Dolly paused with a startled gasp. She was halfway across the yard, peering through the mist, squinting and shaking.

"That didn't sound like no raccoon."

She had lived in the Bluff Creek area for nearly twenty years and heard nearly every animal noise there was to be heard, but she had never heard any sound like that before. She wasn't even sure if it was an animal, but whatever it was definitely came from the . . .

Trembling, she aimed the flashlight beam toward the clump of trash cans—and the noise.

"All right. Who's there? You'd better scoot, whoever you are, before I . . ."

The beam bounced erratically across the glistening metal cans as they fell over, tipping into each other as something darted behind them. Another loud shriek chilled her to the bone as the beam caught a glimpse of dark fur and reflective yellow eyes.

"What in—?"

Then the flashlight died in her shaking hand. She shook it, then smacked it angrily.

"Oh, no. Not now. Not . . ."

She glanced up and saw two glowing, yellow eyes staring at her from behind the trash cans, close to the ground.

"Stupid raccoon!" she cried.

Suddenly, the two glowing, yellow eyes lifted from the ground, until they were floating in the dark about seven feet high.

Dolly knew then that it was definitely not a raccoon. The flashlight dropped from her hand and rolled uselessly in the wet grass. She felt her entire body tense and explode in disbelieving horror, culminating in a scream that easily matched the animal's shriek.

Her one conscious thought—the stories are true.

Another scream caught in her throat as she turned and scrambled toward the trailer's back door. Her arms and legs waved about her wildly, the animal's shrieking following close behind.

She flew into the kitchen and slid the sliding glass door closed with a panicked sob. Her heart pounded in her chest, threatening to burst. She struggled with the lock, her fat fingers barely able to push it into place.

Slowly backing away, she stared through the glass into the darkness, waiting for the animal to appear. Her brain exploded with images of the thing breaking through the glass, coming at her savagely. What would she do? Horrifying scenarios played out in her mind as she backed away. She had easily died a hundred times over by the time she thought of a possible salvation.

The phone. Call the police.

She nodded and ran to the phone on the counter by the sink, a rush of relief racing through her at the fleeting thought of rescue. Would the police make it there in time?

She clutched the receiver to her ear, looked up, and screamed.

A monstrous, leathery ape-like face leered in at her through the kitchen window, absolutely motionless, grinning hideously.

The world seemed to end at the sight. Her blood froze. She couldn't breathe. She could only stare at the grinning, deathly face peering through the open blinds.

Stark fear propelled her over the ten steps to the living room.

The car. *Run to the car*, her brain screamed through white bursts of terror.

She grabbed the front door knob.

A large, hairy ape-like arm burst through the door, splintering through and dragging part of the screen door with it.

SLAM! 10-year-old Oliver Tuttle slammed the book shut and tossed it onto his partially open backpack. The cover of the book read *Omah: True Accounts of a Living Legend*, and pictured an enormous footprint above a mysterious silhouette of an ape-like figure. The backpack held about a dozen more books, each dog-eared and reference-worn. Oliver had read them all, more times than he could count.

He could still feel his pulse racing, his heart drumming in his chest from the frightening encounter he had just read. He let out a long, uncomfortable sigh and shifted on the long, green bus seat, trying to block out the carnival-like noise all around him.

Adjusting his thick, black-rimmed glasses and pushing the stray blonde hair out of his face, he stared out of the bus window, watching the trees whizzing by in a green-brown blur. The scenic part of the ride to Camp Omah was over, and the long, winding, stomach-churning part was starting. He knew he would get sick if he continued to read, and that was the last thing he wanted his fellow campers to see.

The other boys and girls were laughing and singing and talking excitedly about the lake, the future cookouts and campfires, the races, and the rafting.

He didn't care. He had other things on his mind. Camp this year was for one thing and one thing only.

This was the year Oliver Tuttle was going to catch a monster.

They've been expecting you.

STRANGE FORCES™

The invasion of Fairfield has begun. Are you ready?

Order now or take this page to your local bookstore!

☐	1-56714-036-X	#1 No Substitutions	$3.50
☐	1-56714-037-8	#2 The Midnight Game	$3.50
☐	1-56714-038-6	#3 Driven to Death	$3.50
☐	1-56714-039-4	#4 A Place to Hide	$3.50
☐	1-56714-040-8	#5 The Last One In	$3.50
☐	1-56714-041-6	#6 Bad Circuits	$3.50
☐	1-56714-042-4	#7 Fly the Unfriendly Skies	$3.50
☐	1-56714-043-2	#8 Frozen Dinners	$3.50
☐	1-56714-044-0	#9 Deadly Delivery	$3.50
☐	1-56714-045-9	#10 Knightmare	$3.50
☐	1-56714-046-7	#11 Something Rotten	$3.50
☐	1-56714-047-5	#12 Dead On Its Tracks	$3.50
☐	1-56714-052-1	#13 Toy Trouble	$3.50
☐	1-56714-053-x	#14 Plant People	$3.50
☐	1-56714-054-8	#15 Creature Features	$3.50
☐	1-56714-055-6	#16 The Weird, Weird West	$3.99
☐	1-56714-056-4	#17 Tune in to Terror	$3.99
☐	1-56714-058-0	#18 The Fairfield Triangle	$3.99
☐	1-56714-057-2	Strange Forces	$5.50

I'M A STRANGE MATTER™ ZOMBIE!

Please send me the books I have checked above. I am enclosing $_____ (please add $2.00 to cover shipping and handling). Send check or money order to Montage Publications, 9808 Waples Street, San Diego, California 92121 - no cash or C.O.D.'s please.

NAME _____ AGE _____

ADDRESS _____

CITY _____ STATE _____ ZIP _____

Please allow four to six weeks for delivery. Offer good in the U.S. only. Sorry, mail orders are not available to residents of Canada. Prices subject to change.

JOIN THE FORCES!

™

An incredible new club exclusively for readers of Strange Matter™

To receive exclusive information on joining this *strange* new organization, simply fill out the slip below and mail to:

STRANGE MATTER™ INFO •Front Line Art Publishing • 9808 Waples St. • San Diego, California 92121

Name _____ Age _____

Address _____

City _____ State _____ Zip _____

How did you hear about Strange Matter™? _____
_____

What other series do you read? _____
_____

Where did you get this Strange Matter™ book? _____
_____